The Rose's Revelry

A Maeseloria Novella

Sandra Hults

Copyright © 2022 Sandra Hults

All rights reserved.

ISBN:

DEDICATION

To the close of old journeys and the beginnings of new adventures. Thank you to my husband, my daughter and my girl. You have been my support through the roughest of times. I love you all.

1

Lily Eisen's water broke all over the foyer's marble floor. How Marc Jade managed this little miracle south of Mornesse baffled her. This was her home, their home. Hot, sharp tears clouded her vision before another contraction struck. Less than a second later, he was beside her. This man that had promised her everything, and delivered. "My lord," She gritted her teeth as pain rattled through her body. Lily could handle pain. She was the pride of the Guild. These contractions were unlike anything she had ever experienced.

Her pregnancy had not been awful. The discomfort was the worst later on. For someone who moved with the night's grace, walking like a duck was an embarrassment to her training. As her pregnancy advanced, she had taken to skirts over fatigues for reasons of comfort. Marc had only once commented about her more feminine appearance. His tone and his choice of words earned him her daggers in their headboard. That meant he was not welcome in their bed. After a week, she forgave him and let him back into their rooms.

Distantly, she heard Marc curse then look hard at Layla and Brona. "Hot water, towels, both of you. Expect family to show up soon." Marc barked instructions; his voice edged with concern. He felt the pulse and presence of his children more often for the last few months. "How long have you been in pain and didn't see fit to tell me, my heart?" The moment she woke up this morning, his Lily had engaged the wards on her engagement ring. Lily's stubborn, independent streak was evident in the action. Her pain has started that morning. Marc sighed. Now was an inappropriate time to discuss Lily's stubborn streak. "It doesn't matter. Let's get you upstairs." *Alex?* Months ago, Lily had insisted that Alex be the one to assist in birthing their children. Right now, Marc needed his sister's steady comfort.

"I'm already here, Marcus." Alexandra spoke behind him. She anticipated his need, as she often did. She understood that her steadiness would keep him from panicking. "You've done well so far. Let's get her upstairs. Lily-love, I need your rings disengaged." A second later the ward was gone. Marc almost dropped his wife because another contraction hit. A moment later, the sensation eased because Alex lowered his pain receptors. "Thank you." He muttered. Memories of Alexandra's labor with Kira surfaced. He remembered being curled in a ball in the fetal position for the better part of twelve hours. If he were being honest, the memory was hazy with a mix of pain and brandy.

"I want to be conscious for this." Alexandra, Fate love her, shared nothing of their shared experience.

Minutes later they were in the master bed chamber. Marc made quick work of the skirts his Lily had worn that morning. He swapped the blouse for one of his shirts at her request. The last thing he would ever do is deny Lily what she wanted right now. "I'm here, Lily." He bent over and stroked a lock of dark hair out her face. Marc settled on the edge of the bed to offer what comfort he could.

"You Fate-damned better well be. I'm not doing this without you, my lord." Lily cursed and then burst into tears. The room fell into an awkward silence because tears were so rare for Lily Eisen. Her tears mixed with frustration, pain, and a bit of embarrassment at her hesitance.

"I should've married you months ago. I'm sorry." She tensed as another contraction tore through her. Lily did not scream through her contractions. Most women would have and not a single soul would have blamed her. Lily's Guild training taught her pain management. She also didn't feel Marcus lowering her pain receptors enough to cope. "Now, can we do it now?" The confused look on Marc's face made Lily want to sob. Was he so uncertain of them? Had she waited too long? "Now, my lord. I want our children born with your name."

Marc's expression bordered on misunderstanding and laughter. Of all the times to choose their wedding day. He supposed their family was hardly conventional. In that vein, Marc reached out to the only person he would have asked to officiate. *Old man? Can you? The rings are in my rooms at the palace. Not everything has been moved yet.* Marc blew out a breath and leaned over Lily. Nicholas agreed without hesitation. His agreement chased the tension from Marc's shoulders. The old man was the closest thing to a father Marc ever had. "If you are certain, my heart then I will do what is necessary to make it happen for us. Alex, can we build that bond and have her in labor at the same time? Will it hurt the twins?"

Alexandra smiled. "No, not at all. That bond is between the two of you and will not impact them at all. I will numb yours and Lily's pain receptors during the ceremony so you can focus on the two of you rather than her care. I imagine Nicholas will be here as soon as he finds the item you asked him to." Lily and her brother bonded during childbirth. Feeling that second hand made Alexandra's heartache with regret. She wished Nicholas was present at Kira's birth. Only Tessa had aided her through childbirth. Marc had not known what to do with himself.

Heat bled through the room with her husband's arrival. The elemental reaction was not uncommon when he and Alex were in the same room. *All was as Fate meant it to be when Kira was born, little one. I was not ready then, not for this or your heart.* His chiding brought color to her cheeks. *I would not trade this moment for a reversal of our past, beloved.*

"Now what is this about a wedding and a birth on the same night?" He teased them both gently. His teasing became outright laughter when Lily glared daggers at him. Delaney would have his hide later, he suspected. "It would be my honor, little mother." He murmured to Lily before approaching the bed. Nicholas tossed Marc their wedding rings. Marc had purchased them with the engagement ring before he asked Lily to marry him. Nicholas understood that certainty. "I've already blessed them, my boy. I thought we might be short on time."

Alexandra lowered their pain receptors enough that Nicholas could begin. She listened as he spoke the incantation would bond the couple in each of Fate's cycles. The power that built in the room in response echoed of her own. Alexandra breathed through the spike and pushed the extra magic from the room.

"Fate bless thee in this life and all that follow." Nicholas murmured and pushed his blessing into their joined hands. They repeated the vows older than Nicholas himself. He was proud to marry them and equally proud of the man Marc was growing into. "You are now man and wife. Fate blesses your union today and always. Kiss the bride, my boy." Nicholas grinned. "Before she starts cursing your existence."

Marc settled into her mind with ease. The brush of his lips centered Lily, as he knew it would. The moment was difficult to start their bond together but he would trade that for nothing. Lily wanted to be his wife. Whatever difficulty they faced in getting there, he would endure without complaint. That included labor pains his wife was currently experiencing. His wife was beginning to feel her contractions again. "It's almost time to push Lily. Where are the girls with the towels and water?"

As if summoned both Layla and Brona stepped into the room with the requested items. Layla stumbled at the new bond between Lily and Marc. That and a moment later, the force of Lily's latest contraction swiped at Layla's mind. Alexandra almost giggled at how fast Layla put her mental walls back up. "It's okay, little one. This is part of the process. Everything is going as it should. You just missed your mother finally caving and marrying your father." Alexandra's tones were cheeky as she guided Lily to the foot of the bed. "It's almost time, dear heart." Alex ran a soothing hand along her sister-in-law's calf.

"About damned time, Mom," Layla muttered as she set the towels down to Alexandra's left and Brona set the basin to the Sorceress' left. Layla took up residence on Lily's opposite side. She summoned a small cloth and wiped the sweat from her mother's brow. "You're doing great Mom, don't stab him right now. Later...if you still feel like it." Layla crooned. This was a life neither one of them could imagine for themselves. A home, a family, those things were Lily's fondest dream. Layla blinked as she felt the flicker of familiar presences downstairs.

Layla noted with no small amount of pride that her aunt already had matters in hand. "Nicholas love, could you go down and greet Ariana and Jaylor? I imagine Emma and Edward won't be far behind." Nicholas did not answer his wife in voice or thought.

After giving a soft blessing to the newest additions to blesses their family, Nicholas exited the room. "Thank you, Nicholas." Alexandra murmured. Nicholas's anxiety bounced around the back of her brain. He worried she would falter, that their loss would prevent her from being present. She understood better than anyone in the room. Her loss, her inability to conceive again haunted them both. "We have matters in hand. I promise you." Her reassurance held a degree of finality. Her brother needed her. Her sister-in-law needed her. Nothing would keep Alexandra being here, even her trauma with the subject.

Christine Elizabeth Jade arrived squalling into the world. Minutes later, her twin, Daniel Alexander followed her. Both twins had a mop of Lily's dark hair. The force of Fate's blessing in them told her their eyes would shift later. To what, she could only guess. She blessed them each the moment she helped birth them. Fate gifted them this day. She washed them, then wrapped them each in a quilt. Alexandra handed Christine to Marc first then Daniel to Layla. "You did beautifully Lily."

Alexandra took the time to heal any tears that Lily experienced from giving birth. She could not alter the body's natural process after birth but she could prevent pain. She soothed her sister-in-law and gave her a little extra energy.

Alexandra wiped her hands on a free cloth and sat back to appreciate the work she had done. *Someday, beloved. Someday Fate will bless us again with another.* She thought to Nicholas downstairs.

Joy masked the sadness of her memories. Alexandra would not accept any other outcome to the day. "Brona, can you go downstairs and tell our guests everything went well?"

"Absolutely, Alex." Brona said and darted out of the room. She felt like hell at the moment. Her stomach rioted because of the magic that saturated the room. It was all

Brona could do to keep breathing. Thank the Light she had not eaten before her arrival. Then again, that might have been part of the problem. The moment she set foot out of the chamber, she almost collided with her grandfather. "Excuse me Papa-" Brona pushed by him and ran for the nearest basin. Thank the light there was one near her mother's chamber. Her grandfather's cool, firm hands brushed her hair back. When she finished, she flushed bright red. "Too much--"

"I know, Rae. I know. Your grandmother was the same way. She was magically sensitive. I apologize that I did not think to ward you so you would not suffer." Nicholas helped her stand. The moment Brona wobbled on unsteady feet, Nicholas scooped her up from the floor. "Didn't eat, did you? Layla's going to have your hide, little one." Nicholas teased and pressed a kiss to her brow. "Let's get you downstairs. Edward and Emma just arrived. Did everything go well?"

Brona nodded. "They're beautiful. Their names are Daniel and Christine Jade. They've got Mama Lily's dark hair. And Christine has Layla's lungs because she was raising hell when I stepped out." The power in the house made it hard for Brona to keep her eyes open.

Soon enough, she was set on a sofa downstairs. "No magic, no healing. Just peppermint tea and toast. I'll be fine once all the magic tones down." She said the moment Emma Jacobs reached for her magic to soothe Brona's nausea.

Emma acquiesced to Brona's knowledge and left to go get or make the items Brona requested. Brona breathed. As she did, she saw grey and brown fur rubbing against her shins. "Smoke." She murmured and lowered a hand to rub his ears.

The wolf had taken a liking to her the moment they met. Instead of adding to the burden of magic around her, he eased the air around her. Brona blinked. A second later Brona grinned and patted the couch beside her. "I won't share your secret if you won't." Smoke thumped his tail and sprawled across her lap until Emma returned.

"Everyone upstairs is fine. I think Marc will be down to greet you eventually. Mama Lily is well. Alex handled the birth and, if you missed it, Papa Nicholas married them, finally." Soft laughter greeted the latter remark. Brona laid her head back on the sofa and closed her eyes. Her head pounded. She had the same problem when she visited the capital or Vincenzo estates. Too much magic, the presences that came and went were too strong, too defined for her to handle.

So far, the only family home she did not have that backlash was in the North with Tatiyana and Dominic. No one could explain why this happened to her, either.

All her grandfather would say was that her grandmother was the same way. The situation frustrated her. Rather than focus on her annoyance, Brona tried to quell the pounding between her ears.

Emma returned soon enough with the requested tea and toast. "After we settle your nausea, we can treat your headache, can't we Nicholas?" The cleric's question was curious. Emma had no context for Brona's sudden illness.

"You can, just get her stomach settled first. Her grandmother was sensitive like that. I should have warded her when I arrived but matters escalated too quickly." Nicholas was sheepish for the first time in many years. Emma's glare was enough to chide him. The last thing he needed was Emma chastising him when he felt guilty enough. "I know, I know. I feel awful enough Emma." He muttered.

A rock sat in the pit of his stomach. Alexandra's parting thought held so much hope but Fate only knew what was in store for them. His beloved little Sorceress could not take another loss. She and Marcus relied on one another when using their magic. They would find it difficult if Alex were to become pregnant again. Nine months of neither one of them touching Fate's gifts would be a trial. Nicholas would not trade Alexandra's safety, physically or mentally, for that of a babe in the womb. If Fate gifted them, that was her blessing but Nicholas would not actively seek such complications.

After a few bites of the toast and a few more sips of tea, Brona could open her eyes and see the world in normal color. "Okay, I can handle that healing now, Emma, if you would. No, Papa Nicholas, your magic is too close to mine." She said when he offered to help. "Stop feeling guilty for not remembering a woman's reaction. Her life was long before anyone in this room was even a thought." Brona smiled when her grandfather flushed to the roots of his hair. He did not take chiding well. A few minutes later, Brona settled on the couch.

Smoke continued to play lapdog, pressing himself as close as he could get to keep her calm. She caught her grandfather's concern that she might be missing out on meeting the twins. Brona paused to reassure him. "I will go back up and see the twins when the magic settles down. I'll be fine." The longer she sat in this magical chaos, the more she suspected she might make her home in the North. The sudden sadness she felt from her grandfather earned a scowl. "Out, Papa Nicholas. It's not like you don't visit Lochton two or three times a month as it stands." Brona chided him as she pushed him from her ind. "What I plan to do will have me traveling much of the year anyway. You won't lose me so soon after finding me." Brona reached over and grasped his hand in hers. She gave his fingers a gentle squeeze. "It will all work out according to Fate's grace. You'll see. You've waited too long for these blessings."

"That is Fate's truth." Jaylor chimed from across the room. He, Ariana, and Edward kept to the other side of the parlor so they did not impact Brona's recovery. His little dancer and her Knight's control were by no means weak. He, like Emma, had no context for Brona's sensitivity. Ari was almost as controlled as Tatiyana. "I'm glad to see you upright, cousin. I understand why you did not stay long at my home. Before your next visit, I'll have Uncle teach me how to lay a ward against your skin to keep you safe. You're family after all." The warmth in his words soothed Brona and earned her gentle smile.

"Thank you." She said while rubbing Smoke's ears. Brona glanced at Emma and offered a little grin. "Smoke's kind of attached to me, is there any reason?" Brona appreciated the loving warmth that Smoke offered without reservation.

All Emma could offer as an explanation was a small shrug. Smoke's behavior had changed since Alton passed. She understood that her direwolf was a magical null. Emma could only begin to understand what Fate and Alton's last wished blessed Smoke with. "I can guess it has to do with your relation to another Devereaux he knows and loves. He said something once about your family having an affinity for wolves."

She glanced at Edward and the others. Her smile was warm but not sad. "I can only stay for a short time. Elys is in the capital with her Uncle Aries and Aunt Evie. They dote on that girl. Baby Xavier is her best friend. He lights up whenever she's near his cradle. The boy takes a shine to her for some reason."

The fond smile on Emma's lips ached of a mother who very much loved her offspring. Elys would never doubt her family loved her. "You owe us a visit, brother-mine. Bring Joce next time."

Alexandra spared Edward his sister's teasing because she joined them downstairs. Layla was hot on her heels because she felt Brona's sudden sickness. "Lily is ready to see some of you. The babies are both healthy and snuggled up with their mother. She asked for you first, Jaylor, Ari." Alexandra funneled her power down to nothing. The exchange between her husband and Brona out in the hall had not escaped her notice. "Forgive me for unsettling you, Brona. The situation."

"The situation could not be helped and he forgot to ward me. It's all right, Alex." Brona finished the statement with a smile. If one more person apologized to her for a situation beyond their control, she was going to start screaming. "I'm glad everyone's healthy. I'll go up after Jaylor." That was when Layla wedged her way onto the couch between Brona's opposite hip and the arm of the couch., Smoke was not moving to accommodate anyone.

"Are you okay?" Layla blurted the question while Brona sipped tea and rubbed Smoke's ears. Worry etched its way across Layla's brow. She knew Brona had bolted from the room a little too fast. Mom had noticed too. Her sensitivity was part of Brona's magical heritage that they were still trying to understand. Lily never had to ask Layla to go check on Brona. Then again, their mother never had to ask Layla to do anything when it came to Brona's care. Layla was out the door as soon as Lily and the twins were settled.

"I'm fine, just fine. Too much magic. Emma and Smoke here took care of me. Papa Nicholas feels like hell because he didn't think ahead." Brona buried her annoyance behind her mental walls. Her care was important. That need should not detract from the two little blessings upstairs. "How are Mama Lily and the babies?"

The two women settled back on the couch to discuss the new lives. As they did, Smoke crept across Layla's lap to get her scent. Brona spoke in blunt words with her sister. Once their mother and the twins established a routine, she needed to leave Mornesse. She outlined her plans to her sister. Layla would settle for nothing less than her full itinerary. "I plan on settling in Lochton eventually. It feels the least magically charged. So," Brona grinned. "You'll just have to get used to the cold."

Jaylor and Ariana left the room while Layla complained about the cold in Lochton. The protest sounded halfhearted at best. Layla would agree to whatever Brona needed. "Come on little dancer, let's go meet my grandchildren." The word felt so foreign in Jay's mouth that he struggled to digest it. She credited him with raising her but the reality was they grew up together. He was only fifteen when she entered the Guild. Still, he had taken her under his wing the minute he met her wide, green-eyed gaze. At first, he was still recovering from the hurt of Elize's loss. Over time, Jaylor learned to love Lily for herself.

"Stop being morose. Today is a joyous day. Fate has blessed our family." Ariana squeezed his hand to draw him from his reflections. "I have something to tell you after you meet them." She murmured. This moment was for Lily and her babies. Still, Ariana had her own news to share once matters stabilized. His curious expression earned a grin and brought a brilliant light to her sapphire eyes.

The moment Jaylor touched her hand and did a mental check on her health he would know. *My little dancer.* He thought as he examined her in the ten seconds before Marc answered his knock. *You hide better than I do. You can depend on us talking later, among other things.* Jaylor's thoughts were husky with warmth. They would go home immediately unless Lily saw fit to house them while she became accustomed to motherhood.

"Hey, Little Bit," Jaylor murmured as they stepped inside. Lily was half awake and both twins were passed out on either side of her. The cradle made him smile when he passed. He could feel Alexandra's blessing and how the woman had made an allowance in the cradles' wards for him. *Thank you, Spitfire. For seeing my daughter through this and protecting them all.* He sat on the edge of the bed with Ari at his side. The little girl at Lily's side woke the moment the bed shifted and looked up at him with bright, expectant eyes.

"Father-mine." Lily murmured softly and cracked an eye the minute Christine stirred. "Your granddaughter requests the honor of your presence. She's been fed so she shouldn't kick up too much of a fuss." Lily felt him lean close before he picked Christine up. He brushed a soft kiss across her forehead as he so often did as a child. "Love you too, Father-mine. Stay the week with us. I need your security. I'm scared I can't do this."

Jaylor's glare shut Marc's mouth. He understood Lily's fears better than her husband. A father's prerogative, he suspected. Jaylor softened his voice to reassure her. "You can do this, Lils. I promise you. You have a loving heart no matter how hard you protect it or hide it. Trust yourself. You did right by Layla, you'll do right by these two." Then, he scooped Christine from Lily's side, nodding that Marc should do the same with Daniel. "Rest for now. We will look after them until they need you again, won't we Dad?"

Marc smiled. "Of course. Rest, my heart." He kissed Lily softly then collected his son. A father, he was a father. He shared Lily's terror. His hands, after all, were not clean. He helped raise Kira in the old man's absence but this was different. "Hello Daniel." He murmured and brushed a kiss against the top of the baby's head. "You felt the wards?" Jaylor nodded as he laid his granddaughter down. "Enable them as soon as they're both down." Marc explained as he laid Daniel down. Immediately, Christine began to fuss about being away from her mother's warmth.

Jaylor snickered. He took a guess, picked Christine back up, and laid her down beside her brother. The girl immediately settled down and went back to sleep. The men enabled the wards. "Well, that answers that question. Do not separate twins." He whispered with a little laugh then thought about Ariana. "I suppose that's good to know." His eyes met Marc's again. "I'm going to figure you'll have rooms set for us by sunset, right?" The smirk that crossed his best friend's face was answer enough. "For now, let's let them all sleep. Emma and Edward will come up and bless them in a little while. Em will understand the need for them to rest."

Jaylor and Ariana left the room. As soon as the door closed behind them, Marc mentally clicked the lock shut. He was taking a nap with his wife at this point and no one was going to stop him. Sitting in the back of her head while she hurt like that made him itch to see her safe and hold her close. No one in the family would have understood his feelings except the general himself.

Aries weathered two births with Evelyn. Marc shared Lily's exhaustion even if his fatigue was only mental. Fate above he did not know how the women in their family survived giving birth. He only felt echoes of their contractions and the pains of childbirth. Those echoes made him want to run for the hills.

Marc could guess by the smug look on Ariana's features that she had a huge secret she was keeping. The only other person that would've been privy to that secret was her Knight. Ari could not exactly keep that from Edward. A few minutes later he tucked himself around Lily. Wrapped in one of his shirts, she was sound asleep. Marc pressed a kiss to the back of her shoulder and, soon enough, he dozed too.

In the hall, Ariana led Jaylor into one of the many empty rooms in Marc's house. He had designed the place large enough to house the family on Progress as needed so there were plenty of rooms. Marcus was more thoughtful than anyone in their family realized. For all his brashness, his pride, his arrogance, he loved them all. His protective streak dug him into holes that he often had to get himself out of. Over the years, Marc learned to curb that inclination, Ariana noted with pride.

"Now what's this about something to tell me, little dancer." Jaylor swept his wife into his arms and down the hall away from the family downstairs. He knew. The moment he checked her health he knew. How could he have missed that change in her? He swept her into an easy waltz down the hallway. The step was one of the first she ever taught him. The laughter in her eyes tormented him as it often did. He dipped his head and murmured against the shell of her ear. "I do have ways of making you talk."

Ariana answered his whispered words with an unladylike snort. "You wouldn't dare, Jaylor Vincenzo and you know it." The amusement in her tones was clear. Ariana knew her husband better than anyone walking this realm. "And you know exactly what you felt." She matched his steps with ease. Of all the dances she knew this was her favorite because of their shared history. "One boy, one girl, due late Isean." Ariana murmured up at him. "Corrine Elize and Nathaniel Aries." Jaylor missed a step at his daughter's middle name. Ariana covered his mistake. "I wanted to honor the sister you lost so long ago, Jaylor."

"You..." Jaylor could not find the words to express himself at her decision. The room blurred with his tears as he spoke. "You make me the happiest man in the realm, little dancer." They concluded the dance and he dipped his head and kissed her until she melted against his frame. "Now, how about I plan a little mayhem with that brother of mine." Jaylor reached to see what his elder brother was up to. Aries was the first person he wanted to share his joy with.

He saw that his brother was watching Robert puzzle over some problem his mother had presented him with. Xavier was sound asleep in the cradle. Jaylor reached and mentally smacked his brother upside the head. Their promise to Christi prevented outright bloodshed between the two siblings. That did not stop Jaylor from needling Aries whenever he felt the moment was appropriate. *You will be an uncle before the end of next Isean. Do make sure you are at our house when our children arrive. Give Evie my love and tell her to keep you out of trouble.* Jaylor grinned when he heard the distant rumble of Aries laughter.

Jaylor could only hope that Robert would be as close with his little brother. Out of everyone else in the realm, there was no one he would rather have at his back than his big brother. He knew Aries felt the same. "Now what do you say to finding a bed chamber to call our own? We both know Lily and Marc will let us choose whatever we want, anyway."

Ariana's jaw dropped at his suggestion. For a moment, he thought she would refuse. Her surprise drifted into an imp's grin. "I might have already discussed the matter with Alex." Jaylor blinked. He supposed Alexandra would have been the one his little dancer trusted most. The Sorceress was also the best equipped to keep secrets from him. "I wanted someone to check my health just to be safe and I didn't want you knowing before, I was sure. I'm about a month along, no morning sickness. J-Jaylor!" She screeched when he scooped her from the floor and carried her down the hall. No one would have interceded, not in this house.

Emma barked a laugh as she saw her brother turn as red as his hair. She felt how fast he shut the mental doors between himself and his Sorceress. "That bad, was it? I heard her squeak upstairs." His nod was answer enough. Emma could only imagine Edward's discomfort. After all, Jaylor and Ariana were not shy about their flirting or their love life. "That must be a blast…" She teased him as she linked their arms together. "Smoke, stay with Brona for now. We'll be leaving soon to go get Elys." The direwolf was one of the last remaining links to her beloved Alton. At her instruction, Smoke almost wiggled himself off the couch.

Not only did he dote on Elys, but Robert was also by far one of Smoke's favorite playmates. She spoke to no one of her other predicaments.

Two weeks ago, Smoke herded a large female stray into Sierra's shop. The dog was pregnant with pups. Emma guessed that she would be due in the next few months. What on earth was she going to do with a litter of puppies? Emma had no clue. She could guess what Fate planned but the direwolves were a new blessing. One, she was certain, would go to Elys and the two could grow up together. The others, she would have to see.

Edward nudged her. "Sorry, sidetracked by a problem back at Sierra's." Emma said. Edward sensed her distraction. He always did. "Let's get those babies blessed so you can go home to Jocelyn. Dinner next week, beloved, or I'll come looking for you in Mornesse's palace." Her laughter answered her brother's scowl. "Or worse, rat you out to you your fiancé." That had her brother muttering curses beneath his breath. As children, their mother would have blistered his ears. "Glad we settled that." She grinned as they crept into the bedroom.

She felt Marc stir long enough to disable the wards on the cribs. *Go back to sleep, dear one.* Emma murmured and gave Marc's mind a little nudge. If Marc were fully awake, Emma could not nudge him back to sleep like this. Marc's latent abilities would never allow her interference. Alexandra was no different. She could only guess that was part of their gifts from Lady Fate.

Emma leaned over the cradle and whispered to Edward. "Mother said you and I were no different. Do you remember?" Her brother's smile was gentle as he looked down at the newborns. "Fate bless your children, welcome them into our world with love, peace and an abundance of your blessing." Emma whispered. Holy's grace lit the room for but a moment. She took care not to disturb anyone in the room.

Edward echoed his sister's prayer. As of late the twins rarely worked magic together. Adulthood drove them to different corners of the realm. Edward's hand on the small of her back helped with the magic's drain on her body. His presence always gave her gifts a much-needed boost.

Since Alton's death, major magics were difficult for his sister without Duty in hand. Healing she managed. She could give her blessing but the strength seemed to dampen over time. Edward did not know why and did not ask. If Emma knew, she wasn't telling him. They slipped from the chamber out into the hall. Edward, if he were being honest with himself, refused to think about why. The truth was too painful for him to contemplate. "Would you like me to escort you back to the capital?" Edward offered with an easy grin.

She would reject his offer. He also suspected his sister would not mind the help with a teleport. "I haven't seen my niece in a month or so." His words earned an elbow in the side. "Ow." Elys Winslow had her father's dusty brown hair and her mother's striking green eyes. She was almost a year old. Her favorite words were 'Mama', 'Smoke', Gamma, and 'Juice'. Fate blessed the child with her father's easy-going nature. Emma felt that her stubborn streak mixed with Elys' nature.

Elys was not contrary but once she made up her mind, the child would not relent in that decision. The attitude amused her grandmother and exasperated her mother to no end. "We can see if she's learned to say 'uncle' yet." Edward murmured. The toddler knew him and ran for his arms since she learned to walk but the word 'uncle' was not quite in her vocabulary. Elys was learning fast.

"You'll just have to see when we get there, won't you, Edward." She teased as they proceeded down the stairs arm in arm. "Alex, could you re-enable the wards on the cradle?" Emma asked the moment they hit the foot of the steps. She saw Alexandra sat on the floor in her husband's lap, resting against his chest. Emma felt the distant pull of Alex's magic and how the wards went up.

"Thank you." Emma shot the couch a look, where her wolf sprawled out as if he owned Brona's lap. "You, get down. It's time to go." Smoke whined and flattened his ears in protest. "Now." Reacting to Emma's tone, the wolf leaning up to lick Brona's cheek before he hopped down. He rubbed against Alexandra then moved to sit at Emma's feet. Her wolf had a fondness for their Lady of Light that Emma never understood either. "Give them my love when they wake, would you?" She owed Lily Eisen more than she would ever admit. Lily helped her bring her brother home. The circumstances at the time were far from ideal but without her, he would not be standing beside her.

After Alexandra agreed to deliver that message, Edward laced their fingers together. Emma grabbed Smoke's collar and the three of them vanished from Marc's new home. They reappeared outside the palace. Alexandra's wards prevented them from teleporting into the palace. She understood the security decision behind the wards. "Smoke, find Elys." Neither twin knew their way around the palace but Smoke would find his way by tracking Elys' scent.

A few twists and turns through the palace halls brought them to the Redwynds' door. Before Emma could knock, Smoke sat back on his haunches and howled. The door barred him from his quarry. Through the closed door, Emma heard her toddler shout "Smoke!"

"Here we go." Emma murmured. "She rides him like a horse lately. And you allow it don't you, boy?" Smoke chuffed his agreement with Emma's assessment and wagged his tail. "Don't you dare!" Aries was not opening the door fast enough. So, Smoke howled again. This time the sound was loud enough to pierce Emma's eardrums. "Fate damn it, Smoke. Must you?" The wolf whined and, a moment later, Aries Redwynd filled the doorway.

"No patience, that one." Aries grumbled as the direwolf pushed past him to find Elys. The child had ambled her way off Evelyn Redwynd's lap. He swept Emma up in a tight hug as soon as she got through the door. "Good to see you. Come to check on my Eve, have you?" Aries teased. The man and the general, Emma felt, were often two different men. It was a necessity Emma understood. "Okay, fine, you came to see Robert too." Aries grunted when Emma socked him square in the shoulder. Emma stepped around her to look for Elys.

"Mama!" Elys noticed her and Edward's arrival once she finished rubbing Smoke's ears and hugging him. The child ran for her mother's arms. Her sun rose and set on this child. Emma understood that from the moment Sierra laid Elys in her arms. Emma scooped Elys up with a laugh. "Nap or no nap?" Emma asked.

"No!" Elys informed her cheerfully. That was when her daughter noticed Edward. "Unca!" She shouted and dove from her mother's arms. The letter L was still difficult for

Elys. At the sudden shift in Elysia's weight, Emma lunged to the side. Edward rushed to catch Elys before she toppled out of her mother's arms to the chamber floor. His interception was successful. Emma's arms ached from the jerking motion needed to keep Elysia in her arms.

"Well," Edward said after settling Elys in his arms. "That was almost a disaster." Laughter edged his voice as he settled Elys against his chest. "I can help with that lack of n-a-p." He spelled the word to avoid the toddler's ire. Only once had he visited when the little girl was stubborn about her nap. The child was hell on wheels. Evelyn stood and ushered him to a rocking chair near the balcony.

The knowing smile on her lips told him she knew exactly what he was about. He flapped a hand at Emma to go speak with the Redwynds.

Emma wrapped Evelyn Redwynd up in a tight hug. Xavier's birth was difficult for the petite woman. Both she and Alexandra fought to keep mother and son alive during a long, arduous labor. "How are you feeling?" Examining Evelyn's physical health was the work of a moment. But, Emma understood, motherhood was much more than a woman's physical health.

"Tired." Evelyn grumbled. "Xavier doesn't have his days and nights straight yet. He'll figure it out." Her voice was half-hearted at best. As a baby, Robert was a good sleeper. He was an easy child, an unintended blessing. Xavier had a mix of his father's will and her temper. More often than not, Eve saw herself in Xavier's emerald eyes.

Emma watched the woman with a smile and thought to Eve beneath Aries' mental hearing. He has his mother's quick mind, doesn't he? Evelyn's smile was answer enough. Emma surmised Evie would indeed have her hands full with young Xavier. You will have all the help you could ever ask for. Bring him North to me if you need a break and a nap. Aries was an attentive father but sometimes children needed another woman's touch. "I had something I needed to speak with you both about. I had an ulterior motive in asking you to watch Elys. But first, the good news. Labor went well. Lily, the twins, and Marc are fine. I suspect Jaylor shared some news with Aries as well." The glare Evelyn shot across the chamber at her husband was priceless. Emma restrained the urge to giggle before she disturbed Edward's efforts to get her daughter to sleep.

Emma watched as Aries flushed before his wife's scrutiny. He then rushed to explain the news Jaylor had relayed to him. Evelyn was going to be an aunt twice over. "I blessed the cradle and left them with the receiving blanket you knitted for them, Eve. Now, the other motive." Emma outlined her situation with the pregnant dog at Sierra's shop. "I would like Robert to have one of the pups. You know what a companion Smoke has been to me. I would like him to have that if you'd both allow it."

Aries froze at her suggestion. He was a frequent visitor to Emma's home in the North and Sierra's shop in Lochton. Aries was doing what he could to preserve Alton's legacy. The truth of Alton's death limited his choices to honor the man. Memories flickered through Aries' mind. The public at large could not know the truth. That was what Christiana decreed. That was one of the very few arguments he had with the Queen over the years.

In the capital, Aries commissioned a statue in the man's honor in the palace gardens. He created a position for deserving officers as the "Queen's Shield". The position was far from an honorary one. Christiana needed protection. So would her heirs. Unofficially, Kevin Breighton was the last person to lead the Queen's Guard. His death left the position vacant.

His request might not come to fruition in this generation but Fate only knew what the future would hold. The woman that married Devin might need the protection. Hell, Devin might himself. Fate could only know. Aries would prepare for the future as best he could. The Queen's Shield would be responsible for the Guard at large. The Guard would answer completely to the Shield. The Queen's Shield could, if needed, break ranks with the military at large. "I would be honored to let Robert have a pup." He agreed, pulling his mind from his future plans.

Robert, who paid little attention to the conversation froze at his father's last sentence. "Pup?" The boy repeated. He was old enough to understand and, Aries felt, his son would benefit from a companion. That pup would be with him his whole life. Aries could not ask for a better blessing for his eldest son. Aries nodded and explained what was happening. The smile that split Robert's face was worth any inconvenience owning a puppy might cause.

"You'll be responsible for his care, Robert. Do you think you can manage that? Aunt Emma can teach you all you need to know about caring for direwolves, can't you Emma?"

Aries spoke to his son. As he did, he crouched before Robert and met his eyes. The boy was his image right down to the stocky size. Aries remembered being solidly built when he was a little boy. Robert was no different. *Grandma Bri, you would have loved this boy.* Aries thought for a moment. Brianna Taltos would have doted on both his boys, he suspected. Aries wished there was someone he could ask other than Nicholas. His uncle's eyes reflected so much pain that Aries felt it a matter better left alone. "Emma how long until the pups are born?"

"About three weeks from what I can guess." She answered him. "There's a learning curve for pups that I didn't expect. Robert, you can come for the delivery if you'd like but you won't be able to take the puppy home right away. Is that all right?"

Robert nodded. This was the first time anyone had entrusted the care of anything to him. At that moment, she watched Aries come to life in Robert's face. The little boy asked what he could do to help with the puppies. Emma smiled. "Well, if your mother and father approve, you can come stay with me in the North. You can help me with them until they're ready to go to their new homes."

Robert's eyes widened at not only the idea of having a pet. He had never left the capital. He would be away from his parents and the family that so often doted on him here in the capital. He was nine now and itching for a bit of independence away from the palace. The only time he felt he could be himself was around Kira. For the longest time, it was just the two of them as playmates. Their group grew when Devin came along, then Elys. Elys was a baby and not any fun. His mother chided him for saying so when the girl arrived. The problems he had been working to solve when Emma arrived were his penance. Robert turned a pleading look to his mother.

Evelyn laughed, reached, and ruffled her son's chocolate-shaded hair. "Yes. Yes, you may." When the boy cheered, she gave him a firm look. "I expect you to be on your best behavior and I will hear about it if you are not." Robert stopped, flushed, and nodded. Evelyn's approach was more relaxed than her husband's. But she expected a certain degree of decorum when her children were guests.

"I think we will get on just fine, won't we Robert?" Emma smiled and extended a hand to him. Robert needed independence from the crown and all that being a royal child entailed. She never faulted Evelyn or Aries for their choice to keep him here in the capital most of the time. Robert would have room to be a child with a child's adventure and curiosity during his time in the North. Emma would not settle for anything less. When he sat beside her, she hugged him and pitched her voice low. "What color do you think your puppy will be, my boy?"

"All black with blue eyes?" He spoke. Blue eyes fascinated him because they seemed so rare among his immediate family. Nicholas Taltos had the bluest eyes he'd ever seen. His Aunt Christi's eyes were pretty too. Robert was stuck with plain old boring brown eyes.

"We shall see, won't we? Pray to Lady Fate and see what happens, my dearest." Emma hugged him and pressed a kiss to his brow. She glanced across the chamber to see Edward had finally gotten Elys to sleep. "Fate bless you dear one." Emma had been whispering blessings to Robert since the moment she met him. He was a good boy destined for great things. She stood and nodded to Edward, who rose from the rocker with care. "We're going to go home before that one wakes up. She's a mite peckish when she wakes up anywhere but home. Robert, be kind to your mother for the next few weeks. She is very tired and busy with your brother right now, okay?" Robert's solemn nod prompted Emma to ruffle his hair.

Minutes later the twins were out the door and beyond the palace wards so they could teleport to Emma's house. As they walked, Edward offered to stay the night with her in the North. The company was one she would welcome. She added she would invite Sierra up from the city to join them for the night too. The idea of her loved ones around the table eased and saddened her at the same time. *Even now, I miss you so.* Her thought was sad and loving at once. She ached for Alton every day. In her way, she had never stopped grieving his loss.

The last time she remembered sensing his presence was the day Elys was born. She felt him reach through the veil to push a rebellious lock of hair from their daughter's face. *You did well, my love.* She remembered his thought and the warmth of his presence in her mind. Her heart ached at the memory. There would be time for their reunion but that was years off from now. Instead, she would raise and love Elys in his honor. Emma would teach the healers who would follow in her footsteps and she would wait.

2

The following weeks seemed to fly by. Xavier Redwynd settled into a normal sleep schedule. He was the least fussy baby Emma had ever encountered. However, parts of his personality echoed Elys'. When the babe knew what he wanted, he persisted until he got it. That trait, she suspected, was courtesy of his father and would serve to annoy his parents to no end until he managed to master that part of his personality himself.

The direwolf pups were due any day now. Emma and Sierra agreed that it would be best if they moved the mother to be out to her house beyond the city gates. Emma kept a small stable and horse for when she needed to travel and could not teleport. At times, she just took her mare out to ride. Elys celebrated her first birthday just two days ago. At the moment, her daughter was fast asleep with Smoke wrapped around her like a living blanket. That sight was not unusual.

Robert remained in their house since Elys' birthday party. He enjoyed the freedom of being away from the palace. Still, Emma noted how much he missed his parents. "Let's go exploring." She said to him one morning to distract him. "We can go check on mama and then maybe you can help me with the gardens. We'll see what buried treasures we can find in my herb garden." Robert loved checking on the mother to be. Sierra had named her Charity.

The name was a jest between she and Sierra. Both women knew it would have taken an act of kindness to accept their odd, well loved, direwolf. Smoke was set in his ways. His naptime with Elys was the only time she ever got away from the house without his supervision. Alton's last order to him had been taken to heart. That promise now included Elys. "Get your gloves and coat and we'll go. It's starting to get cold. This might be the last chance we have to harvest or go digging in the dirt. In fact, it may be one of the last times you get to water the plants, my boy." He perked at the idea.

Emma wanted to encourage Robert's magical growth. The boy had an affinity for water. He was too young for healing just yet but Emma would work with him on the basics of warding. By the time she was his age, she could manage simple warding techniques and almost all manners of mental gifts. In this, Robert's education was lacking. She did not fault his parents for that.

Aries' troubled history with his magic caused many problems when Robert was a toddler. Evelyn too knew little about raising a child with Fate's blessing. So, Emma intervened when she could. Robert had a freedom in Lochton he could not have at home. There were no wards that might rebel when he used his power. Thank Fate, his emotions were not tied to his skills. He was a Taltos. His gifts required conscious effort and focus.

Emma would have her dose of emotion related powers as Elys grew up. She would have no element to contend with but she was still waiting for her daughter to get upset enough to knock herself unconscious with Holy's gifts. That day would come. For her, that day came when she argued with Edward about one childhood slight or another. She barely remembered the fight, just the outcome. They were so angry at each other that Emma drew enough power to knock them both out.

"Auntie Emma, what's that sound?" Robert interrupted her memories with a curious question. They had just left the house and were headed towards the stables where Charity was housed with her pups. The late Adryn wind carried a distinct whine to Emma's ears.

"Well, let's go and see, perhaps it's time. Did you pray for a safe delivery like I asked?" The boy nodded and fell into stride with her. At nine, he was tall enough to meet Emma's eyes. He would be a giant like his father. Often, she caught glimpses of Evelyn's loving heart. As they reached the stables, Emma smiled. "It is time. Can you run up to the house and get some blankets, my boy? The pups will need the extra warmth with the late Adryn cold." Robert took off running before she could finish asking. His excitement was palpable. Emma did not expect him to comprehend the work that lay ahead.

Minutes later he ran back with his arms full of the old blankets she intended to use for this occasion. She had shown him weeks ago which ones she would need for the birthing. "Now Robert, when they come, they're not going to look like what you'd imagine a puppy would. It takes a couple of weeks for them to even open their eyes. The best we can do is help keep them and mama warm and fed during that time. It's our duty to keep them safe. Do you understand?"

When Robert nodded his understanding, she continued. "Sit down by Charity's head and pet her ears. She will appreciate the comfort right now." Emma instructed on gentle tones. Her stables kept most of the wind and cold out but newborns of any species were such precarious things. She remembered feeling three pups when she checked Charity last. After the first hour, a familiar chuff and inquiry came from the stable door. Clearly Smoke had herded Elys out here. He lifted his head over the barricade that kept him from Charity and the pups. He whined at Emma as she worked. "You cannot help, dear boy. Just wait it out. I've already sent for Mama Sierra from the city. She'll be here soon enough. I also summoned Tati as soon as she's off rotation to come help with Elys." The shuffle of his paws on the stable floor was enough to indicate his satisfaction with her answers. Such was often the way with she and Smoke. He stopped being Alton's wolf the day he died when her beloved entrusted her care to the creature.

Thirty minutes later, Sierra Winslow arrived and peered down at Emma. "How are they coming along, my dear?" At her arm she had a basket of food and provisions to see Emma and two hungry children through the trial at hand. She felt Robert perk at mention of his Aunt Tat, as he called her. The boy did not see enough of their extended family, Emma thought. She would address the matter with his parents when he was ready to go home to the capital.

"Slow and steady Mama Sierra. What is Elys into?" She said without looking up. Emma heard her daughter toddling around in the distance and Smoke's anxious growls in her wake. Her wolf was trying to heard Elys away from a potential danger. She heard the sound often enough as Elys got older.

"The stable holding your mare." Sierra answered, amused at her granddaughter's precociousness. She set the basket down and moved to scoop Elys up. "Now what would possess you to go in there with all the muck when if you'd come to see me, I'd have let you pet the mare with help."

"I wanna do it." Elys stuck out her bottom lip in a petulant pout. "I big enough." Sierra resisted the urge to roll her eyes. Elys' current argument with both her mother and grandmother concerned what she was old enough to do and what she was not. Aside from Xavier, she was the youngest of the generation. She was often left in the dust by her older cousins. The problem was a source of immense frustration for the little girl. Yet there was nothing anyone could do but give Elys time to grow up.

The pout was eased when Emma clucked her tongue down the hall as she helped deliver the pups. Her mare, which had been with her since her original journey at Alton's side, stuck her head out of her stall to be petted. Elys was placated by the horse's warm mane. "Maybe your mother will take you out for a ride in a couple days, dear one. Can you be a good girl until then?" Sierra murmured in Elys' ear. The child nodded. "I'll hold you to that deal Elys. Are you hungry?" The mention of food captured the toddler's interest. Sierra carried her back to the picnic basket she brought. Sandwiches and fruit for lunch. Sierra fully expected that Lady Jade would pester their cook for dinner before she arrived. If Emma was right, the pups would be born when Tati reached them.

Sierra knew Emma would be exhausted by nightfall.

That came with the duty, Sierra understood. A healer's work was often the longest and hardest. Sierra knew this from experience. The toil a healer dealt with was never-ending. Sierra did not have Emma's magic but her role within the realm was no less crucial. Sierra was the one who oft reminded Emma that she needed rest or needed to eat, or sleep when she ran herself ragged.

The people of the North often came to her for care or advice or any number of problems that Lady Jade could not manage. Sierra lost count of the number of sick children that crossed Emma's doorstep or arrived at Sierra's shop in search of Lochton's Cleric, or that was how they dubbed her when her name escaped them.

At sunset, a trio of squeaks cut the quiet of the stables. Three pups, one black, one white and one cinnamon colored that had Smoke's white-tipped ears. "Two girls and a boy." Emma announced. "And the boy is black." She looked up at Robert and grinned. "We'll just have to see what color his eyes are in a couple weeks. Emma wiped her brow and grabbed the towel Sierra handed over the barricade. "Thank you, Mama." She murmured. Robert perked when the black pup made his entrance into the world.

"Onyx." Robert said with a small smile as he watched the pup root at his mother's breast to eat. Charity looked exhausted. She never nipped at him or bit him for being so close while she worked to bring her babies into the world. The birth was one of the most beautiful things he had ever seen. When the male pup finished feeding, he started crawling for Robert's knee. Charity growled and plucked her pup back to her side.

Outside the partition Sierra had picked Elys up to show her the babies. "Look, little one, the puppies are here." Elys squealed and looked down at the tiny bundles. The white pup, when she heard Elysia's voice, turned and started to crawl towards Elys. "I want that one!" Elys announced as she pointed at the little creature approached her. That, Sierra, suspected, was Alton's final wish at work. He told Smoke to "take care of his girls".

"In time, my dearest." Emma said softly. "You have to let them grow up a little first. I can teach you how to feed them when they're bigger and can open their eyes." She wondered if that was part of Fate's blessing to Smoke when Alton passed. Emma wished she could ask. The reaction from the two pups was certainly unusual. The babes were no bigger than her palm but, she suspected, they would grow like weeds. Smoke had.

"How did it go?" A quiet voice interrupted the commotion into the stable. Tatiyana filled the doorway and, just as Sierra predicted, had a large basket on her arm from the Devereaux kitchens. As usual, her sword, Hope was belted at her hips. Her ash blonde hair bounced in a fat braid against her back. Life in the North was calm, calmer than in most other places throughout the realm. Still, Emma noted, Tati was never without her sword. Often, Fate's Chosen kept their weapons within reach or on their person. To be separated was difficult for the weapon's owner.

Emma's curiosity was answered the moment Tatiyana spoke. The cinnamon pup started to crawl towards the sound of Tanya's voice. Emma chuckled. "Quite well. In a few weeks, my dear, you may have more than you bargained for. One of these little darlings is yours." Emma's laughter cut the quiet. "She just tried to crawl to you when she heard you speak. All the others have done the same. So, logic dictates. Come have a look."

Tanya blinked a moment then passed Sierra the basket she had brought with her. Their cook was always happy to provide for more than just she and Sion. She peered down into the straw and blankets to see a dark red little wolf trying to crawl towards her again. "Hello there, little love." Tanya's soft croon made the pup squeak. Her mother growled and tugged the little one back to feed. She had never been responsible for another being in all her life. The room blurred. When she started to cry, snow came. Sion's presence touched her mind so he could ease her heart before she thought to ask for his help. "Wouldn't they be warmer in the house at this point?" She said quietly. "I can move them if Sierra and Robert will go ahead and make a place for them."

Robert was on his feet before Tatiyana finished speaking and hurrying out of the stable. "Mama Sierra, a place in my den should be fine. Take the blankets we didn't use." The elder Winslow laughed at Robert's spirit and followed after him. Emma's instruction was gentle, as it always was. "And you, little miss." She leaned down and brushed a kiss atop Elys' head. "You need dinner soon. Can you ride Smoke back up to the house?"

The words were magic to Elys, who charged the direwolf. Smoke chuffed, wagged his tail and got down enough for Elys to climb on. As soon as she was settled on his back, Smoke took the little girl up to the house. Elys knew better than to squirm on Smoke's back. She only fell once when she and Smoke were still learning. She clutched his fur to hang on but never pulled hard enough to do any real harm to Smoke. As they left Emma could hear Elys' giggles in the yard. As soon as they were alone, Emma met Tanya's eyes. "I miss him every day."

Tanya reached out and hugged Emma tight. Fate knew her heart bled over Alton's loss every day. Yet, they both kept on. "I know, Em. I know. I think about him often and how proud he'd be of you and little Elys. This, this would be more than he could ever have dreamed of." That was when Emma started to cry. She was exhausted and the pups' birth had hit just a little close to home. Tanya let Emma cry for a while.

So much of the family expected her to be at peace with Alton's sacrifice. They treated her as if she was done mourning. Tanya knew grief did not work that way. The emotion assaulted you when you least expected. "Let it out. You know Elys will try and come back. Rest," Tanya pressed a kiss to Emma's temple then reached for Robert in the house. *Is everything ready, my boy?* Like Emma, Tanya encouraged Robert in his gifts until they would be almost intuitive. The advantage was one Aries never had the opportunity to learn. Tanya learned by force and survival. She pushed the thought aside. Now was not the time to dwell on her mother's madness.

All set, Aunt Tat. Grandma Sierra said to set up the blankets in the den near the hearth because they needed to be warm. Can you see where we put them? His thought was clear and the dear boy thought if he concentrated harder, Tanya could see what he had done to see to the puppies' care. She smiled. Had she and Sy ever been so innocent in their gifts?

Lighter touch, you don't need to force to let me see, my dearest. Just look at what you've set up and I can see just fine. Good work, love. Then, one by one, mother and pups disappeared from the stable and reappeared where Robert had set their new homes up. "There we go, now they will stay warm against the Isean chill. Let's say we go inside and have dinner, rest and wait for the next feeding session in a few hours?"

"That sounds wonderful. So does a bath and a set of fresh clothes. Births are always so messy." Emma said with a sigh.

"Yet the outcome is so much better than a fight." Tanya teased before she wiped Emma's eyes and the two women left the stables.

3

In Mornesse, Lily struggled to adjust to motherhood. Brona and Layla were less depending on her than the twins. Their needs exhausted her but she still made time to learn her husband's magic. She would never attain his fluency but that was not why she wanted to learn. The lessons helped them grow closer. No more ghosts stood between them.

Lily often struggled to discuss certain necessities of Guild life. Missions sometimes required a certain level of intimacy with the target. That was her life before Marc. What she endured brought her husband's rage. She would always remember the way the hearth burned blue that night. Trusting him enough to share those memories helped him understand her issues. "I'm sorry I made you wait so long." She murmured one night as they lay together wrapped around one another.

Before they laid down together, the twins fell asleep after another round of feedings. How they ate so much Lily would never understand. Layla was Fate's gift these last few weeks. This morning, her daughter traveled to the capital to meet the Queen. Christiana wanted Layla's help reviving

Morningstar Stables. The business offer was lucrative and involved Layla doing what she loved. Since the first night Lily took her daughter to the Guild stables, horses were Layla's passion. She had an affinity for animals that made Lily smile. "Isn't Alexandra and Nicholas' anniversary soon?"

Before he answered her question, he addressed her apology first. "Waiting for you was the most devastating thing I ever experienced. A woman has never made me wait until you. If anything, the time taught me to be patient and act with care when it came to your heart. More than once I learned a lesson at the end of your blades." Marc pressed a kiss to the back of Lily's shoulder. "Or your father's fists." He grunted when Lily dropped an elbow into his ribs. "I'll thank you for not trying to break them this time, my heart." He felt the gears turning in his wife's mind. As he detected her train of thought, he grinned. "It is, what are you thinking?"

A smug little smile curled her lips as she wiggled back against his body. "A joint ceremony since they never had a formal one and neither did we. Are you interested in keeping secrets your sister?" Marc never turned down the chance to surprise Alexandra. Such opportunities rarely presented themselves. Their connection to one another did not allow for those secrets.

"Hmm," He murmured as his wife pressed close to him. She was going to derail his train of thought at this rate. "If you'll hold still, I can think, Lily." Her response to his request was the press of her bottom against his hips. He sighed and nipped her shoulder in retaliation. "You're terrible but I love you. I'm in. I suppose this comes with all the trappings of a typical ceremony. Not seeing your gown, distracting the old man as needed and blocking my sister?"

"That's just the start of the list, my Lord." Lily explained on lofty tones as she rolled over to face him. Her eyes sparkled with mischief as her plans solidified. "I understand being worth the wait but you both deserve a celebration with the people that love you." Lily tucked an errant lock of ash blonde hair behind his ear. "Consider it my apology for making you wait until the day our children were born." Her lips curled in a smile before she leaned up and kissed him. "For tonight, I guess you can persuade me to entertain you." Exhaustion licked at the edges of her mind, but the warmth of Marc's touch always seemed to energize her. He laughed and rolled her beneath him to distract her instead.

The next morning, Lily worked to feed the twins before she started reaching out to the family network to plan the ceremony. Their ballroom would suffice for both ceremony and celebration. Afterwards, Lily would need to plan a feast with so many magic users present. Marc added a ballroom to their estates so they could host Progress for their family. Jocelyn's castle was too close to Madryn's book for the comfort of Fate's blessed. Jocelyn also did not want to have that type of security risk so close to Madryn's book. Lily understood the Princess of Mornesse's concern.

"What is it, little one?" Christine cooed up at her mother. As she suspected, the twins had their father's eyes, and his chin. Christine inherited her mother's resolute streak. She had her mother's stubborn streak. Fate help them all when she became mobile. Both twins were already rolling on their bellies without help. She had just adjusted her shirt and set them down to wiggle on a blanket when a knock sounded at the chamber door. "Come in."

When Jaylor Vincenzo stepped in, she smiled. "Just the man I needed. Come sit with me a bit, Father-mine. Marc and I need your help with something." As she spoke, Daniel was rolling his way towards the edge of the blanket with a determined little scowl on his face. "No, you don't you little sneak. That floor is cold, you will not be happy." She scooped him up, nuzzled his cheek with her nose until he giggled then set him back next to his sister. Christine was drooling and watching the fire.

"What is it you needed, Lils? You know if you need me, I'm yours." Jaylor sat down on the floor beside her. He smiled when Lily leaned into his side. Her happiness was contagious. The moment she outlined her plan, he sighed. "You are the second person in this family to ask me if I can help them work around our Spitfire, do you know that?"

Lily laughed and grinned up at him. Aside from his expression, her bond with Marc allowed her to sense Jaylor's presence and his love for her. "Because you're so damned good at what you do, father-mine. Who was the first?"

"My uncle when he wanted to propose to her. I had to break into her chambers in the palace to get her engagement ring." Jaylor huffed as he hugged her. His complaint was half-hearted. The spark of mischief in his brown eyes betrayed his true feelings about the request. "Now you want me to work around them both to get them a surprise ceremony for their anniversary. I suppose I'm supposed to act as an intermediary with the rest of the family, aren't I?" His mind was already working on the problem. In fact, he reached for his little dancer and drew her into the conversation to listen. *Help me with the feminine parts of this planning. I am utterly clueless, little dancer.*

Five minutes later, another knock sounded at Lily's chamber door. The door swung open and Ariana stepped in. "I had a feeling you'd be joining us once he heard my request." Lily smirked then sat up so her father could greet Ari. "Are you going to be in on this too?"

"Of course, who else can help you manage a gown. I also know Alexandra's sizes without poking around her head." Ariana said as she sat down beside her husband. The moment she did, Christine decided it was time to move and scooted towards Ari. "Well, hello there, little darling. Come to see me, have you?" Christine chortled the moment Ari picked her up to tickle her sides. "I would also recommend sending Marc, to get her roses from the Jade manor gardens. The violet and white ones are special to her. Nicholas managed to get them the day they were wed. She never told me what was special about them. I only know she was very touched by his choice of flowers. Tati has a connection in the North that can help get corresponding flowers to match the bouquet. I'm sure she'd be more than happy to help us since we will be sure to invite Dominic."

Ariana smiled over at Lily. "We can't have the best man not at the wedding now, can we?" Then she grinned up at her husband before blowing raspberries at Christine. The babe chortled in reply. "I suppose you'll be performing the ceremony, again."

Jaylor heaved a sigh and looked at the ceiling. This was going to come back to haunt him. He knew it. "I haven't even agreed to do anything yet. Fate save me from plotting women." This earned him a poke from both women in his life, one at dagger point. Jaylor cursed and rubbed the newest pinprick in his side. "Damn it Lils. Who taught you--" Jaylor laughed and refused to finish his question. "You know what, never mind. I know who taught you. All right, I'm in. I reserve the right to take Marc and my uncle out to get them shit-drunk the night before. Maybe I'll even drag the big bastard with us." He mused. "So, what do we need to do first, ladies? I am yours to command within reason."

They set about the morning planning the ceremony, the décor and how Lily would manage both the event and the twins' demands. The trio debated how exactly they were going to work around the realm's foremost telepath. The woman was often in and out of Lily's home as she pleased. The feat would be difficult to pull off. Marc would do his best to distract his sister from all the new life among their family. Kira reaching her early teenage years helped his cause.

Kira wanted to see more of the realm. Alexandra was working to accommodate her daughter between royal duties. Often, the limited time led to clashes between mother and daughter. The time would come for Kira to step into her mother's shoes. With Fate's grace, that time was still years off. Kira needed training to undertake before she was ready. Her trials to become a full-blooded Sorceress would take all her cunning and bravery to win. She had no inkling of who her knight would be or if she would even have a Knight.

Lily juggled lists and plans and decor with motherhood. The anniversary was in a few months so they had time to prepare. Her twins learned to crawl on the ballroom floor. More than once, Ariana came sailing in, scooped them up and danced with them around the room. Lily used this distraction to manage a particularly perplexing problem. Christine adored these visits while Daniel tolerated them. He loved time with his father or when his half-sister came to visit. Layla was also helped with the planning and often ran errands for her mother. The event was coming together, Lily noted with pride one afternoon. "Oh no you don't." She snapped and scooped Christine up as she went for the hearth again. "You do love the fire, don't you?" Christine flashed her a gummy smile.

How old would her children be when they manifested their magical talents? She wondered. After the celebration, Lily would have a frank discussion with Alexandra. She was far from mastering Marc's talents. As her children developed, so would she. For all that to happen, she needed at timeline. Only her sister-in-law had a timeline for that development.

Lily could also think of no better teacher for her children. After all, Alexandra taught Layla with an ease that still impressed Lily. Layla could be a stubborn learner, Lily reflected. The girl wanted to know everything right now whether she was ready or not. Alexandra handled that will with good humor, grace and play. Layla learned to play with her power before she learned to wield them with any measure of efficiency. Alexandra taught her that her power was a natural part of her as much as it was a tool. Now that she felt how magic raced through her husband's blood, Lily understood Alexandra's teaching.

The two of them were living, breathing representations of Fate's grace. The title Christiana bestowed upon Alex was more apt than their monarch knew. Alexandra bled Fate's blessing like most people breathed. Lily suspected that power had more drawbacks than her sister led others to believe. Lily knew about the miscarriage and Alex's inability to conceive. She knew that Alex loved bigger than she let others see. Perhaps that was why Lily understood her so well. In that respect, she was no different.

"You are more alike than either one of you would care to admit, my heart." Marc teased from the ballroom door. Gentleness itched in his emerald eyes. "I see you have matters well in hand." He watched his wife with their daughter in her arms. Marc had never been this happy in his life. Christine was her mother's image with her mother's attitude. "Fate damn it." The man muttered and rubbed the back of his head. "I'm guessing she taught you to do that, didn't she?"

"Better than a dagger, my lord." Lily sing-songed as

she spun about the ballroom with Christine in her arms. "Do take your son and join us. He's been a right terror this morning. Didn't want to be held. Didn't want to eat. Didn't need changed and most assuredly...did not want to sleep." To emphasize her point, the moment Daniel caught sight of his father, he started squealing to be picked up. At least, Lily supposed, he wasn't screaming. "See?"

"Now what is all this fuss." Marc murmured, amused at his son's antics. He sat down on the blanket next Daniel. He was kicking his feet and had his tiny fists in the air. The baby kicked and squealed and squawked. When his father did not meet his demands, he scowled and threatened to start screaming. That was when Marc reached over and brushed his fingertips across Daniel's forehead. The confusion written across the boy's face almost made him laugh. "You can't always have what you want right now, my boy. You'll learn though. Come here."

Then, Marc scooped the fussy baby up. "He's teething." Marc said with a small smile. When he touched Daniel's forehead, Marc made quick work of checking his health. A fussy baby could mean just a fussy baby or it could mean something far worse. "I see you have the drool-monster." Marc grinned while Christine gummed a lock of Lily's hair.

"Oh, Fate damn it." Lily grumbled then laughed at

the insanity of the moment. "I've killed men for less and here I am giggling like a loon at her drooling on my hair." The smile on her face was content. She took her free hand and worked the lock from Christine's fingers. "That's quite enough of that, young lady. What do we have left to do to get this place ready? We have, what, a week left?" She asked Marc as Christine reached for another lock of her hair. "I said no." She repeated on firm tones. Christine pouted a moment then tucked her head under Lily's chin. Thank Fate they both were not screamers. "Also, you're giving them and me a bath tonight, my lord."

Marc rolled his eyes to the heavens then laughed. "Hm, do I get to join you for this bath, Lily?" The sparkle in her eyes answered him. "We have a week; I am going to go get the flowers the morning of since Jaylor cannot get by the wards on the house. Alex would think nothing of me being on the property, after all. Did you talk to your father about recreating her gown?"

"Yes. He took care of that almost three weeks ago. It's set. I'm guessing you provided the measurements? You are rather familiar with the feminine form, after all." Lily's smug smile and sarcasm had Marc bursting into shocked laughter.

"That's still my sister, you know." He grumbled at her joke. Fate above, his wife went for blood when teasing him. "Actually, I've sat in on enough fittings to discuss business with my back turned. I have the numbers burned into my memory. Occupational hazard as her Knight." Marc moved close to Lily, his tone sobering. "At the beginning of Christiana's reign, rumors were rife that assassins were coming for Alex. We had to take the necessary precautions."

Marc dipped his head to brush a kiss across the line of Lily's jaw. At least, that was what the twins would allow anyway. "I will gladly give you a bath and take the twins off your hands so you can relax. What were you planning while I deal with our little miscreants?"

"Dagger practice." She answered with a sweet smile that earned swearing from her husband. "Not on you. I need to get my form back and only have a couple weeks to do it. Dagger practice and sparring are my exercises of choice, my lord. You've done nothing to warrant my ire. Or is there something you'd like to tell me."

Marc grinned, then kissed his wife again. "Not at all, my heart. Not at all."

4

Daniel had two teeth burring along his gums the day of the big event. Two days before, Brona arrived to help finalize the affair. She also offered to babysit the twins during the ceremony and the ball after. At this point, both twins were sleeping through the night. Lily caught Brona's reluctance about attending. Lily also understood that Brona's sensitivity to magic prevented her from attending most family occasions. Of her three daughters, Brona was more inclined to solitude. Brona could not grow in the shadows. She needed Light, as they all did.

So, Lily improvised. She put a gown of elegant silk and sparkling stars in the twins' closet. She would have a small chat with Brona before she left the nursery. The shade was a rich navy blue, an echo of her Taltos heritage. Her seamstress created the sparkle using hundreds of tiny faux gems and seed pearls. Lily knew it would likely be the finest gown Brona ever owned.

Alexandra was the last to arrive. As far as she knew, the party was for Lily and Marc. She saw no problems with sharing the day of her anniversary with her brother. Though, Lily knew, Alex looked forward to time alone with her husband. *She'll get it.* Lily thought with a wry smile. *Just not in the manner she suspected.* The smile on her lips earned a curious smile and a question. Lily shook her head. "Nope, no questions Alex. Just trust me." That was when Lily pulled her own gown out of her closet. She paused then pulled out the replica Alexandra wore on her wedding day.

"You didn't." Tears filmed at the corners of Alexandra's eyes. "You aren't. Little sister, my darling Lily...did you?" For once, the eloquent Lady of Light could not find words. The air warmed around her as she hitched in a calming breath mixed with a sob. She could not afford to lose control, not now and not during such a beautiful moment. Her heart pounded while panic tugged at the edges of her mind.

Lily saw the concern and immediately worked to address the problem. *A moment, my lord.* Lily murmured in Marc's mind. Then, she engaged the wards on her engagement ring. Before Alexandra could protest, Lily wrapped her up in her arms. "I did. We did. You deserve every happiness. You should celebrate your union with the people that love you, Alexandra." Lily pressed a kiss to Alexandra's temple. "Now calm down or you're going to end up going down there all blotchy and a certain someone will think I made you cry." Lily leaned back and tipped Alexandra's face up to her own. "How about you and I get ready for this day like the sisters neither one of us ever had?" Minutes later, Alexandra found a smile and, thank Fate, her skin cooled.

In another part of the house, Nicholas stood next to Marcus. The young man was settling into his suit. Marc asked Nicholas to wear his best suit and stand with the boy for his big day with Lily. "What are you about my boy?" Nicholas asked, amusement trickling into his tones. "You've been looking like the cat that swallowed the canary all morning." Nicholas teased. That same moment was when he felt Alexandra's power and emotions spike. "I suppose I will do your sister the courtesy of not prying into the answer she already has." He funneled the excess power off of his wife and did not press the issue. He could guess, if pressed to do so. If this were what he suspected, Christiana would finally get her wish.

Downstairs, the monarch in question helped put the finishing touches on the ballroom. The flowers were perfect. Jaylor and Aries rolled a cloth of fine white linen out along the ballroom floor for the couple. Everyone in their family helped. No one wanted to miss either ceremony. "Cousin, how can I help?" Christi let out a joyous whoop at Jocelyn's arrival before embracing the woman. The two had become quite close since her brother's failed coup. Jocelyn grew into the capable, fair ruler that Mornesse needed. Her cousin was the leader Christi suspected Jocelyn would become.

"I didn't know you were coming. No one told me." She shot Jaylor a dark glare. At the same time, her Shadow found the flowers in his hand very interesting. Christi caught Jaylor's smile when he looked away. "I see who the culprit was, don't I, Joce?"

"You do indeed. How many people in the realm would have the audacity to plan around you Christiana?" Jocelyn teased as she returned Christi's hug. The women worked with the others to get everything set up. Marc did not have a chapel on the property. That was an addition to his lands that he had not addressed yet. He would address the matter or Tess and Alexandra would flip a coin for his hide.

An hour passed while everyone dressed. Alexandra and Lily, once dressed, checked in on the twins a moment. Lily met Brona's eyes with a firm expression. "If you are feeling brave tonight, check the closet, little heart." She hugged the girl but did not explain anything further. Brona's curiosity, Lily suspected would win the day. Lily was counting on it. "Let's go get married, shall we? I hired a very specific little flower girl to precede our arrival. Jaylor is awaiting me at the top of the stair." Lily flashed Alex a grin. "I arranged a special escort for you since you have no parent to stand with you. He was quite insistent on his role too, I might add." Alexandra's puzzled expression made Lily want to laugh. She knew that would become clear in a moment. The two women left the nursery and the twins to Brona's care. Lily knew her babes would be fast asleep within the next ten minutes, if that. They were groggy when Lily left the room.

Brona's curiosity did overcome her fear about their

family overwhelming her. She opened the closet and almost wept at the waterfall of silk that tumbled out. "Okay, Mama Lily. I hear you." She said as she began to dress. Brona lulled the twins to sleep with a small lullaby as she dressed. Brona pushed the smallest of compulsions into the song. The extra mental push would help the twins sleep the night through. "Your escort is at the bottom of the back staircase, little heart." Brona blinked at the note once then twice in confusion. Still, she followed Lily's instructions. Once she was ready, she blew out a breath and touched her fingers to the Taltos crest at her throat.

At the foot of the back stairs stood Sion Jade, flanked by Tatiyana and Layla. The three looked up at her and smiled. Sion offered his arm after Brona embraced Tanya then Layla in turn. The women's affection for her was clear. Sion was still a mystery to her. His interest both frightened and flattered her. All she knew of men began and ended at thirteen. Few men felt safe for her.

Throckmorton, that bastard was still haunting her long after he was gone. When she reached the foot of the steps, Sion offered his elbow. Tati and Layla linked arms and headed for the ballroom. "Hello, Brona. I am happy to see you." Sion murmured as they walked into the ballroom. Their family was all seated and waiting.

Brona passed an impatient, impeccably dressed Kira on her way in. "You look lovely. Be patient sweetheart." She clucked Kira's chin with her free hand. The girl was far too big to scatter petals on the linen walk way. Brona suspected that Lily exchanged the basket for a tasteful bouquet of flowers. Brona loved all the realms children. They each had a fondness for her. She travelled often enough right now to visit each of them. "I can't fathom why you would be happy to see me, my lord." Her tone was cool until Sion laid his hand over hers. Then, she trembled. The warm contact was patient and kind. Brona fought the urge to flinch. She recovered and murmured as she sat beside him. "We've barely exchanged twenty words since we met."

The set down prompted Sion to burst into laughter. "I would change that if you would allow me. It appears we're starting. I'll be quiet before I draw any further attention to us." He teased as she blushed. Heads turned when he laughed. She noticed before he did. Fate help him if he could not get out of his own way tonight.

At the top of the stairs, Lily and Alexandra greeted their escorts. Jaylor was a given for Lily but his companion earned a broad smile from Alex. "I had to, Lexi. I couldn't have you doing this alone." Aries Redwynd scooped Alex up in a tight hug. "You don't mind, do you? I mean, you've been more my guide than the other way around. You helped me find who I was meant to be in Fate's grace. I will be forever grateful for that." He paused. "I was also told to give you this before we entered." Aries pulled a bouquet of violet roses from behind his back.

Alexandra flushed to the roots of her hair at his compliment. She tried not to cry over flowers but, Fate above, who had done that. A moment later she had her answer. As a result, her brother flinched at the other end of the aisle on his wedding day. "Well, she got her flowers." Marc muttered and rubbed the back of his head.

Nicholas laughed because he knew exactly what flowers and when Marc had gone to get them. His beloved had puzzled over the reasons her brother would be visiting the family estate. In his pocket, Nicholas carried seeds from those very plants. He intended to deliver them to North and his dear friend's capable hands. If anyone could make them grow outside of the estate, his friend could. That was when Dominic dropped an elbow into his ribs and whispered. "Could you not in a room full of telepaths, old man? We've kept her safe this long."

"Have faith in my walls and the wards on my wedding ring, dear boy." Nicholas teased right back. "Shouldn't you be harassing your Mate right about now?" Tatiyana had walked in with both her siblings and Brona. Nicholas laughed when Dominic's expression shifted at the sight of Tatiyana. Dominic's entire attention was on the way emerald silk hugged her slender frame. She piled her hair in a loose chignon that accented her face. She was laughing at something her brother said or some discomfort at Sion's expense. His niece sat beside Sion so that assumption could have gone either way. "You're drooling." Nicholas made as if to hand Dominic a spare handkerchief. The old man laughed when his best friend prodded his side.

"Your turn is coming, old man. Just you wait." Dominic murmured with a small smirk. *Hello little warrior. You look exquisite tonight.* His attentive purr through Tatiyana's mind brought color to her cheeks, he saw. *I'll enjoy divesting you of those feminine trappings later.* Then she looked up and stared him square in the eyes. Her message was quite clear. *One dance with you, one with our beloved Lady and one with my niece. Then we can make ourselves scarce.* He knew they were both reluctant to leave the North, even in times of peace. As a couple, they liked living away from the formality of court and the requirements of nobility. This was a family event, true, but he found himself anxious to get her home. "Here we go. I'll try to catch your jaw before it hits the floor."

Kira led the way forward, walking down the aisle towards her father and uncle. The bright smile on her youthful face was contagious. Nicholas smiled back. *You look lovely, little one.* Nicholas thought. As soon as she sensed him, her expression brightened. *Thank you, Papa.* Then she moved to Alexandra's side of the aisle and took a seat next to Christi. Marc stood beside him. *You chose well, my boy. I cannot fathom a better partner for you.* The thought was for the younger man beside him. Lily Eisen was Marc's match in every way. Nicholas could not be happier for Marc.

Nicholas watched as Jaylor set Lily's hand in Marc's then flashed him an expression of pride. Nicholas understood. If he were giving Kira away, Nicholas would want that partner to be everything that Alexandra was to him. Jaylor murmured something in Lily's ear that earned an elbow in his ribs.

What his nephew said, Nicholas never knew. Alexandra was standing at the opposite end of the linen aisle on Aries Redwynd's arm. For a moment he felt like he could not breathe. The dress was a replica of the one he had married her in. He didn't feel his jaw sag or how Dominic reached over and snapped his mouth shut. Nicholas gaped like a fish at his wife. *Fate above, little one, you…* She was more beautiful than he had words for. Fate knew he had promised to spend his life showing her. *I love you. In this life and all that follow.* Neither one of them questioned his devotion or commitment to her. As he expressed his feelings, the bond between them thrummed and he saw Alexandra flush. The recreation was perfect right down to the violet and white roses in her hands. Nicholas also saw her hands were bare, exactly as they were the day he married her.

"I trust you will continue to care for her heart." Aries murmured with a smile when he surrendered Alex's hand to him. That smile did not touch the big man's brown eyes. He was deadly serious in his statement. Aries grew into a man no one trifled with. Nicholas understood the man's protective streak.

Nicholas flashed his nephew a smile. "In this life and all that follow, my boy." He gave her hand a gentle squeeze then tucked it into the crook of his elbow. Nicholas forgot Aries the moment he met Alexandra's eyes. Sea shade bled into emerald. He could feel the heat of both her skin and her power. He funneled both away as almost a reflex. "I know, little one. I know." He murmured. "It's what you wanted on our wedding day. Happy Anniversary." Nicholas dipped his head and brushed his lips across hers.

The double ceremony took a little more than an hour between the two couples. Lily only kicked Marc once just before he kissed her. Whatever he said, made her cheeks flame. In retaliation, she hiked a foot back and kicked him square in the shin. *Thank Fate.* Marc grunted then kissed her. "I love you, my Lily." He breathed against her lips. The emotion behind the simple words were enough to relax her shoulders. She forgave him for whatever improprieties existed between his ears.

Nicholas only had to funnel Alexandra's power off once more during the ceremony. Fate knew she would feel miserable if her gifts harmed Dominic. Nicholas cherished the support of his best friend and of those who supported him his whole life long. "Thank you for this." She said to Nicholas. He shook his head and uttered two words in her ear. "Thank Lily." Her surprise ricocheted through his head. "It was her idea. I didn't figure out what was going on until a week ago but I kept my mouth shut for your sake. I knew you wanted this."

"I did." She admitted. The smile she gave him was beaming. "I don't know how she managed it all." Tears crept to the corners of Alexandra's gaze. Her heart thudded at all the happiness around her. They were all here, their family. People that had earned their way into her heart and her grace. People that taught a lost girl what it was to be home, to have people that loved and needed her.

You are our heart, Lexi. What else would we do? Aries was the first one to interrupt her thoughts. *Lily just put the pieces of the puzzle together faster than any of us could have imagined. She's like her father like that. Now get yourself down that aisle so we can clear these chairs and greet you properly.* She laughed and said aloud. "Don't let Jaylor catch you complimenting him."

"What's this?" Jay said out loud and glanced at his sibling. The big man offered a shrug. The couples laughed and proceeded back down the aisle on the warm waves of their family's joy. Once they reached the ballroom entrance, she made sure everyone was standing. Alexandra willed the chairs and linen aisle away. Christiana had arranged the orchestra for dancing. She knew that Lily would make sure that there was food with so many magic users under her roof. Their ball room was not far from the kitchens. Alexandra could only imagine the army of servants Lily must have hired in the meantime. Marc sidetracked her thoughts when he scooped her up and twirled her around, laughing.

"Stop worrying. Stop thinking, dearest sister." He set her back down next to Nicholas. His tone was chiding but amused. "We are happy. Enjoy the moment." Marc grinned as she swatted him. "Seriously, Alex. We've fought and bled and given for this realm for most of our lives. Enjoy this little corner of happy we've built for ourselves."

"I concur." Christiana intoned then spoiled her serious tone by smiling. She offered both hand to Alexandra. The woman took them and squeezed the queen's hands with affection. "In fact," An impish sparkle lit her sky-colored eyes. "I command that the first dance belongs to the newlyweds, or re-weds as the case may be." She bent and kissed Alex's cheek. "He would be as happy for you as I am now. Let the past be what it is, my beloved friend." Christi squeezed Alexandra's hands one more time before turning her back over to her husband. "Orchestra, if you please. You know which one to open the floor with." The maestro was more than happy to oblige the Queen of the realm.

The opening dance was a reflection of the day's joy. Alexandra fell into step with her husband. This was exactly the moment she wanted that day in the catacombs. Time enough to breathe and love this life, this realm they built together. *I love you, Nicholas Taltos. In this life and all that follow, I will always find you. You have my promise.* The world shifted with her promise as Nicholas gave her hand a fond squeeze. Alexandra felt the pull of life's magic within her. Maybe she never would give him another child but they had each other. That was more than enough for her.

Near the end of the song, Nicholas bent and kissed her. "Always little one. Never doubt it." As the song came to a close, Dominic clearing his throat earned a scowl. "Thirty seconds, Dominic, thirty seconds for the love of Light." The grumbled teasing earned laughter from both Alexandra and Dominic. Nicholas looked down at his wife and willed a pair of kid gloves on to her hand. "There, beloved, now you are fit for people." Nicholas kissed her again before surrendering her to his best friend. "Kick him if he gets out of hand."

Nicholas went in search of his granddaughter on a warm wave of his wife's laughter. He found Brona sandwiched between Sion and Tatiyana. Layla had gone to steal her father for a dance. "Thank you for coming, little heart." He murmured and offered his hand. "Dance with me? You can tell me why Sion looks like he got busted with his hand in the cookie jar." The grateful look on the girl's face did not escape him. "I hope you haven't been improper towards my granddaughter, dear boy. Her mother and I might flip for who gets your hide."

Sion turned cherry red before Brona assured him. "He just tried to hold my hand, Papa Nicholas, it was nothing." Nicholas nodded to her explanation and left to dance with his granddaughter. "He's a nice man that makes me feel things I don't know if I'm ready for." She admitted as soon as they were out of earshot. Brona's cheeks were pink. "I sense his element rather clearly when I am around him and I don't understand why. You know we're counter-elements." Brona let him lead with ease because she was a beginner with these steps. Thank Fate, this song was slower. She would bet that Christi created the set list with the novices like her that would be present. "I think he believes I need sheltered to a point because of how we first met."

"That would be rescuing Layla, correct?" Nicholas murmured as they danced. "So, he saw you at one of your darkest moments. You had not eaten; you did not know who you were. You were far from the people that love you. I do not say this to chide you, Rae, not at all." He paused to turn her in the dance then bring her back to him. "Sion needs to understand the steel that is under your softness. If he does not, do make him. I have faith that you will. If he is where your heart leads, my Brona, trust it. If you ever needed my blessing, you would have it. Jades love hard. They give everything they have to see those in their care safe. I can tell you if you let him, no matter where you've been or have suffered, your care would always be in the front of his mind."

Brona nodded, still unsure if she wanted to pursue the heated interest in Sion's eyes. As she stood there in the light of her grandfather's power, she understood why she felt Sion so clear in her mind. She felt a small, tiny trace of him in the back of her mind. It was as if a part of his power liked her a little too much and stayed with her. On the one hand it was sweet. On the other, the very idea infuriated her.

"Found it did you?" Nicholas murmured. "I felt it the minute I touched your hand, Rae." Sion's choices about Brona displeased him but the fight was not his to have. Brona was a grown, quite capable, woman. Nicholas did not meddle in the affairs of grown women. It was a lesson that Marcus took years to learn. "Do as you see fit, little one but if you would take my advice. Let him stay and watch who you are. Give him the chance to learn before bouncing him out on his ass."

As the song came to a close, Brona leaned up and pressed a kiss to her grandfather's cheek. "Thank you for the dance and the advice, Papa Nicholas." Then, she left the floor in search of the fellow that had left his trace on her. A trace that Brona, if she were being honest, was not sure if she wanted removed. She kept her grandfather's advice in the back of her head. Could she give him a chance? Brona would be lying if she said the idea did not scare her. She stopped beside the bench where he sat, alone, because his sister had gone to dance with her Mate. "Do you mind if I sit?"

Sion looked as if she had startled him from thought. "No, not at all Brona." He scooted over to allow her room to sit beside him. Sion pitched his voice low, amusement lacing his words. "Am I allowed to be happy to see you now?" Her reddened cheeks had him grinning. Her blush was adorable. Sion reached over to lay his hand on hers. That was when he caught her fighting the urge to flinch. "Is it like that, dear one?" Compassion ached in his words. "Forgive me. I did not know. May I touch your hand?" She gave him the barest nod in answer. Her fingers felt chilled in his. "You will never need fear that from me. I will never touch you without your consent again."

Brona went rigid at his tone. His compassion touched her. That sweetness was not enough to dim her sudden ire. He felt she was too delicate to discuss the facts of her life. "Is it like...what precisely, my lord?" Her voice went deadly quiet. She did not like his assumption or that he looked at her like she was some sort of broken creature. "What have you assumed about me rather than ask me yourself?" She was not ashamed of her past or anything she had suffered to get to this moment. Facts were what they were. After Throckmorton raped her at thirteen, she chose never to know anything about men. For the most part, she struggled with male company in general. Nicholas and Dominic were the only exceptions to that. Those two felt like home in a way that Brona did not completely understand.

"You've known harm at a man's hands. You tense up wherever I move to touch you." Sion said in quiet tones. "It's like everything you are goes into deep freeze the minute I get close and I don't know if I can thaw you. I'd like you to let me but I don't know where to start." The admittance was a vulnerable one from him. Yet, he saw that his words only seemed to infuriate her.

Brona's voice pitched to a low hiss as she rose. Fury made her shake. "The word, my lord, is rape. Do not dress it up on pretty words like 'harm'. The word is rape. I was raped at thirteen. I don't understand what you make me feel, why it might be okay for you touch me if I let you, why you fit me. The truth is I don't know." There were few things Brona hated more in this world than not knowing. She hated the mysteries of the heart because they were never logical.

In a reflection of her current frustration, she hiked a foot back and kicked him square in the shin. His howl cut through the ballroom because the orchestra was between songs. "And if you think that I am some broken, weak little creature, guess again. I am as much a fighter as your sister or mine or any woman in this room you can name. You are damned lucky I am not armed right now. To think I am somehow less because of my experience is insulting to everything I've survived." Brona growled. Then, she noticed the awestruck silence in the ballroom. "Fuck." She mumbled then vanished on the spot.

She reappeared in what would someday be the gardens of Marc's manor. She had a feeling the man would not settle for less than gardens that would rival his childhood home. Even in its infancy, the space was beautiful. Brona blew out a breath as she sat on the edge of the fountain. "Of all the Fate-damned things he could have said! Of all the assumptions he could have made, how dare he assume…"

The shadows coalesced next to her and, a second later, her uncle stepped into view. Brona reached for a dagger she did not have. "I took a chance that you weren't armed, Rae." He did not address her mood right away. Instead, he summoned a heavy cloak and wrapped it around her shoulders. Even in Mornesse, the Isean air had a chill. "Now we can talk about it or we can sit here while you calm yourself. I just did not want you catching a chill. I only have one question. Is the man who put you through it dead?"

Brona saw the red edge the corners of her uncle's vibrant eyes. There was a tension in his spine she had never seen before. Heat also boiled off him in a way that was unfamiliar to her. Until now, she had only ever seen him as jovial and caring. He eased her worries and cajoled her out of her concern most times. Or he comforted her and told her that, with Fate's grace, this too would pass. "He is. Sy, Tati and Layla took care of the fucking psycho that was Throckmorton." She blew out a breath and leaned against him to take comfort in his warmth. "He's been gone but, at times, I still dream about it. I was a child. The rape left part of me that still hasn't healed right. You and Papa Nicholas help. You're the first two men I've ever met that read 'safe' in my head. I hate the assumption that I am weak or somehow broken. I couldn't stand the way he looked at me with pity, Uncle Dominic."

"I can certainly understand and respect that, Rae." Dominic said on quiet tones as he wrapped an arm around her. "If the man was not dead, I was taking your grandfather hunting. He would not stand for your harm at another's hands regardless of how young you were." He felt her relax into his arms. "I can say that Sion likely meant no slight. Now, don't you go and tense up on me or elbow me. Your temper is just like my sister's, darling one. Hear me out. Sion suffered a great deal at his mother's hands. So did my little warrior. If anyone is going to understand your fear, or accept where you are with compassion, he will. I know it doesn't seem that way right now. He has more or less shoved his foot in his mouth and is currently choking on his ankle." The visual, he knew, would make Brona smile.

Dominic hugged her. "What I can tell you is those two have the biggest hearts and love harder than any two people I have ever known. Growing up the only thing they knew of love was from each other and a man who sacrificed his life so my Tati could be free. Ask him if he will share his darkness with you sometime, Brona. Listen to what he has to say. I am not saying forgive him right away, but don't look to give him enough rope to hang himself with." Dominic shot her a smile. "Now, I know that you are feeling overwhelmed because the whole ballroom saw you kick him and screech at him."

Brona paled beside him. The idea that the entire realm knew about her past galled her. "None of them care. Others have survived worse. No one in that room will judge you for what you have survived or limit your ability to grow because of it. If they do," Dominic gave her another squeeze. At times, he marveled at the fact that Brona even existed. "You send them to me or to your grandfather. I won't shed their blood on your behalf. I know how you feel about your mother's methods of resolving her disagreements. I will, however, discuss with them the error of their thinking and see it set right."

"Thank you, Uncle Dominic. I know I owe you a dance still so you can go home with Tati." Her statement earned a bark of laughter from him. Brona straightened herself, removed the cloak and willed it back to the house. "Let's go back so I can fulfill that promise for you. I will come to Lochton before season's end. I promise. I need to make sure Mama Lily and the twins are settled."

"As you will Rae." He offered her his arm and swept her back inside to rejoin the festivities. Dominic would wait to see how matters between Sion and his niece unfolded. He had hope for both of them.

Inside the ball room, a glance from Christi had the orchestra resuming. No one addressed Sion. He felt it better that way. His sister settled herself onto the seat next to him. "You're lucky she wasn't armed. I doubt Nicholas or Lexi would appreciate having to heal stab wounds tonight." Tati settled against her brother's comfortable bulk. "Dominic went to speak with her. What on earth possessed you, brother-mine?"

Sion reddened to the roots of his hair at Tati's gentle chiding. "I believe she misinterpreted my concern, Tati. I have not stuck my foot in it like that since I came home." He blew out a breath and looked over at her. "It makes me worry that I cannot do this. That she's not the one that's broken, but I am." His voice was soft and designed for her ears alone. That statement earned a fast, hard punch to his ribs from his sister. Those would bruise later. "Ow, what the devil was that for, Tatiyana!"

"For your thought that you are undeserving of love because of our history. Which is exactly where your thoughts were going, Sion Alexander. Don't you dare think that. Brona is far from fragile. What would you do if someone dared called me fragile because of what I have survived?" Her voice still held a playful, loving light. To him, it was as if she enjoyed his stumbling. "We all stumble in love, brother-mine. Or have you forgotten how hard I fought Dominic?" The wry smile on her features had him chuckling even though his ribs throbbed. "You're also quite lucky Nicholas is only glaring daggers at you from across the ballroom."

"Could you stop rubbing my good fortune in my face, sister-mine?" Sion grumbled as he watched Brona walk back in on her uncle's arm. She barely spared him a glance. He supposed he earned that and the fury that followed the kick to his shins. "I did not mean to infer that she was weak or broken, Tati. I merely wished to tell her that I admire what she has survived and the she never needs to fear any violence from me. I wanted to reassure her and it came out completely wrong."

Tatiyana said nothing as he spoke. Instead, she toned down their connection and slid into Brona's mind. *Just listen for me. I do not believe he meant to insult you. If he did, he'd have an appointment with Hope or Layla's daggers come the dawn.* Tati sat and relayed what her brother was saying to the girl that captured his interest. *I do hope his folly does not keep you from Lochton's gates. The city and I both miss your warmth, my dear. Sierra Winslow asks after you.* Tanya felt Brona tense as she occupied her mind. *I would never push anything about my brother on you. I would ease any misconceptions you might have. My Mate and I love you far too much for that nonsense. Enjoy your dance with Dominic and please see me for my blessing before we leave just as you always have.*

"Tati has a way with words, doesn't she?" Brona murmured. She and Dominic came apart during the dance, circled one another then came back together. This was one of the first dances her uncle had ever taught her. The pace was medium and easy for a novice to pick up. Tatiyana's compassion soothed her anger. As she listened, the tension left her shoulders.

Dominic flashed her a smile then nodded. "She has a larger heart than any of the family see. She hides her true self behind Hope and her reputation as Lady of the North. I understand her reasons and value that she lets me in to see that beauty underneath. You should too, Rae. I agree with her. Don't let him keep you from darkening our door. I will gut him myself if it comes to that."

"I'd rather you didn't, uncle." Brona said gently. "I do not want anyone shedding blood on my behalf. Trust me to work out my own issues with him, would you?" Dominic relented when she met his eyes as she knew he would. "I can accept a verbal stumble if he meant well. That does not mean I'm going running for his arms or completely ostracizing him." She paused, her lips thinning to a line. "He confuses me and I don't know if it's completely in a bad way. I don't like not knowing things, uncle. You know that."

"I do, I do. Matters of the heart are not things you

learn, Rae. They are things you feel, things you understand with time. Feelings are never concrete. They shift. They deepen over time. I have known Tati since she was a little girl chasing her brother across the snowdrifts in the mountains. The woman she became since that child never ceases to awe me. I adore her. She doesn't love by little measures. Then again, neither do Devereaux. Consider it for me."

As the song came to an end, Dominic swept her from the dancefloor with a practiced grace. He hugged her and pressed a cool kiss to her forehead. She adjusted to the difference between his touch and a mortal's with ease. "Go see my Mate for her blessing, beloved girl. I hope to see you soon." He stepped away from her and into the shadows. *Congratulations old man. Give the bride my love. We are returning home. Go in Her grace.*

Brona wove her way through the ballroom to where Tati and Sy sat. She did not even spare him a glance but, as she approached, they both rose. Tati embraced her and kissed each cheek. "Fate bless you, my darling girl. Go in Her grace and with my pride. Come see us soon." With her blessing, her fingertips lit white with Holy's grace. That was the reason Dominic departed ahead of his Mate. A moment later, the woman was gone, leaving Sion and Brona alone. Awkwardness simmered between them strong enough that she blushed.

"Brona, I--" Sion started and flushed red when she flashed him an expectant smile. "I owe you an apology. I meant to comfort and tell you that you did not need to fear me in any capacity. Harming you would be like harming myself." When Brona raised a hand to stop his apology, he grasped her fingers. He bowed and pressed a kiss to the back of her hand. "I echo my sister's sentiment, Brona. Go in Her grace." Then, before she could respond, he vanished from the ball room.

"Damnable man." She murmured in his absence. *Thank you. I accept your apology Sion. I will try. That is all I can give you right now.* Brona blew out a breath and, a moment later, someone hugged her hard. "Mama Lily, Layla." The two familiar, loving pairs of hands eased the remaining tension in her. "I can't believe you both pulled this together so fast." Her jumbled feelings, for now, were set aside so she could absorb the joy of the moment with people she adored. "You both look beautiful!"

"You were brave enough to come down. I thank you for that, little heart." Lily said as she pressed a kiss to Brona's cheek. "Well done sticking up for yourself tonight. Whether he meant it or not. I hope he apologized or Layla might look to skin him, brother or not." Her tones were not serious. If her mother meant to skin Sion Jade, she would never say a word and Brona knew it. Lily would take care of the matter.

"He's my brother but you are the sister of my heart."

Layla spoke from beside her. The words were honest in her bright blue eyes. "The only thing that keeps me from dragging him out on the yards is your dislike of bloodshed. You can do this, though, little heart. He'll see the heart of you makes you different from us in the best, most beautiful way." Layla hugged Brona too, putting her between the two women.

They used to curl up like this when all three of them were in the Guild. Each of them came so far from those dark days. Brona never thought she'd see Light again or ever understand who and what she was. "Okay, okay, you're the third person to tell me to give the guy a chance, Layla. I'm going to settle in Lochton in a month or two once Mama Lily and the twins are settled. What?" As she spoke, Lily's features darkened. That look on her mother's face tended to mean she took issue with Brona's words. On a day like today, Brona did not want to annoy her mother.

"We *are* settled, little heart. Go with my blessing and Fate's grace. Set out tomorrow if it pleases you." Lily said on firm tones. "I will help you pack if you would like. Fate knows except for your books you travel light." Lily shot Layla a glance and Layla let go. She turned Brona towards her until their eyes met, green on green. "You will not put your life on hold because you believe you are needed here. Visit. Come babysit. Come help me raise them. Do not use this as a reason not to pursue your dreams, my little heart."

Lily tweaked Brona's nose as she so often had when Brona was small.

"Fine, Mama Lily, fine." Brona gave her an exasperated but content grin. "I'll go but I'll come straight back if you need me, okay?" She peered past Lily's shoulder. "Your husband is looking for you." Brona stepped back as Marc Jade approached. She respected him, even liked him a little when he wasn't being a high-handed ass.

The moment Marc approached, he scooped Lily up and spun her about in his arms. "So, my heart," Marc set her on her feet after giving a nod to both girls. He appreciated them stepping back so he could get a grasp on his wife. Brona's warning wasn't fast enough, thank Fate. Lily could have taken him off his feet in a heartbeat if she were of a mind to. "Have I told you tonight that you are the loveliest creature I've ever seen?" He said then dipped his head to kiss her until the room fuzzed around them. Marc loved the way she melted into his embrace.

"Not in the last five minutes." She said when the kiss broke. Lily felt liquid after that kiss. Thank Fate the twins were sleeping through the night. Just this week, they moved the twins to the nursery that adjoined their chambers. Lily was grateful for the time alone with her husband. The separation gave them time to reconnect. The twins consumed a bulk of their day to day lives. "How long do you suppose this will go on until we can sneak away?"

"An hour, maybe two, my heart." Marc informed her in sad tones before he grinned, dipped his head and kissed her again. He had yet to dance with his sister or address their guests. "Here's to hoping half the family doesn't decide to stay the night." He murmured against the shell of her ear.

"You're going to make me kick you like Brona kicked Sy earlier." She growled when the kiss broke. The light in her emerald eyes informed him that her anger was in jest. "Unlike Brona, I am not unarmed, my lord, my husband." Her emerald eyes sparkled with teasing. "I suspect we'd best get back to our guests before I make good on that promise hm?"

The teasing tone of her voice assured Marc that he was quite safe from his wife's retribution. The sudden warmth and flare of power behind him told him who intruded on their privacy. If he were being honest, she was the only one who would have dared. "Yes, beloved sister?" Marc did not tear his gaze away from Lily's.

"Well, Marcus, it appears our Queen is looking for you to congratulate you and your wife. We might be among family but servants do talk." Amusement lingered in Alexandra's words. She could almost taste the frustration rolling off her sibling. It served him right after the years he spent carousing among the opposite sex. "I do believe you could sneak away after this next dance if you were of a mind to. I suppose Nicholas and I can occupy the rest of the family for the duration."

Marc's cursing told her what his wife thought of sneaking away. She would not let him leave Alex to manage the rest of their affairs. "I see." Alexandra continued with a smug smile. "I will see you inside, my dears." Then, Alex left them to their own devices to go in search of her husband and Christi.

Marc looked into his wife's eyes as if to find some measure of relief or sympathy. Lily grinned up at him. "Guess we'll have to wait, my lord." The impish smile on her lips had him swearing again before he offered her his arm and escorted her inside.

The rest of the evening concluded without further incident. Marc tucked Lily against his side as the morning sun crested the horizon. He had made good on his promise of later. Until tonight, Lily was waiting for the other shoe to drop. She expected some measure of reckoning for all the blood she shed to get to this moment. Yet, that reckoning never came. Was it Fate's grace? She wondered. Was it her growth and letting the people in her life love her? Or those that arrived and blew the doors of what she thought she knew of life and love? Fate could only guess. Even then, Lily Eisen counted her blessings. She snuggled into her husband's larger frame and drifted off to sleep.

ABOUT THE AUTHOR

Sandra Hults was born in Toledo OH, where she still lives with her supportive husband and daughter. She is the self-published author for the brilliant fantasy world of Maeseloria. Her first novel in the series, Maeseloria: Birth of Light, was published in 2012. An avid music junkie, she can often be found rocking out to anything from musicals to pop to contemporary and classic rock, especially when she is writing. She also enjoys spending time with her family, going to gaming conventions and catching up on the latest reads from her favorite authors.

www.ingramcontent.com/pod-product-compliance
Lightning Source LLC
LaVergne TN
LVHW052032170826
845678LV00020B/3142

* 9 7 9 8 8 4 7 5 2 0 0 0 3 *